FROG, WHERE ARE YOU?

Sequel to A BOY, A DOG AND A FROG

by Mercer Mayer

A Puffin Pied Piper

For Phyllis Fogelman,
a dear friend, who inspired
the creation of the faded
pink dummy.

Library of Congress Catalog Card Number: 72-85544
First Pied Piper Printing 1980
Printed in Hong Kong by South China Printing Co.
COBE
10 9
A Pied Piper Book is a registered trademark of Dial Books for Young Readers,
A Division of Penguin Books USA Inc.
® TM 1,163,686 and ® TM 1,054,312
FROG, WHERE ARE YOU? is published in a hardcover edition by
Dial Books for Young Readers, 375 Hudson Street, New York, New York 10014
ISBN 0-14-054632-4